THE ADVENTURES OF

Hamish McMoosie

≈

Hamish McMoosie and the Long, Black Umbrella with the Goose-head Handle

≈

This book belongs to

Dedication and acknowledgements

This tale is dedicated to children everywhere

A special thank you from Terry to Mandi, who made the tales
come alive with her wonderful illustrations.

And of course to the folk of the Old City who wholeheartedly entered into the
spirit of the tales, as Bruce Brymer the butcher remarked – "It's all a bit of fun!"

Published 2003 by Waverley Books, David Dale House,
New Lanark, ML11 9DJ, Scotland

Copyright © Text – Terry Isaac 2003

Copyright © Illustrations – Mandi Madden 2003

The right of Terry Isaac to be identified as the author of this
work has been asserted by him in accordance with the
Copyright, Designs and Patents Act 1988

A CIP catalogue record for this book is available from the British Library

ISBN 1 902407 29 6

Printed and bound in Poland

Designed and typeset by twelveotwo

Hamish McMoosie

Hamish McMoosie and the Long, Black Umbrella with the Goose-head Handle

Terry Isaac

Illustrated by Mandi Madden

WAVERLEY BOOKS

The old house, in the very old Scottish city, was sitting quietly, half asleep, warmed by the late September sun. Even the wind had decided to take an afternoon nap and was dozing somewhere far out over the North Sea.

Everything appeared to be still and sleepy – except that is for the bees that were still buzzing away, working and humming bee songs as they collected the pollen from the remaining flowers in the garden. The bees knew that autumn was coming and that cold winter would follow swiftly after that. The collection of honey was a priority. Honey, the bees' staple food, was needed for the winter months to enable the hive to survive to the next year.

Bill, the gardener, had finished his afternoon tea break, and after a quick snooze in the sun under the old apple tree, was busy again, mowing the big lawn and raking the grass cuttings into a neat pile ready for a bonfire, once the grass had dried.

The summer, long and hot though it had been, was almost ended. The apples on the seven trees in the garden were beginning to turn from a yellow-green to a crimson red. The days, were not always as warm as today, but were mostly still sunny. The nights were turning chilly and had a touch of autumn about them. Most of the flowers had finished blooming and had cast their seeds around, ready for the next year.

The strawberries and raspberries had been picked and eaten. Swifts were beginning to call to each other, high in the air, saying that it was almost time to be off to Spain for the winter.

Roderick, the human who owned the old house and the garden, was standing under the tallest and oldest of the apple trees. He looked up at the laden branches that almost touched the ground in great green, red and brown arches with the weight of the fruit and then he looked down at some fallen apples. He shook his head and turned to Bill his gardener.

"Bill, that wind last night brought down a few more apples and they are not yet ripe enough to eat. It's a pity to see them go to waste. There has been such a good crop this year."

"There is no need to fret," said Bill, who knew about these things and usually had an answer to most gardening problems. "All you have to do is to gather up some of the apples and to take them into the conservatory. There you can put them on the top of the big cupboard to finish ripening."

He added that Roderick would have to make sure that he only gathered up good apples, for it was well known among country folk that one bad apple could make the rest go to rot very quickly.

Roderick, who was a writer and did not know very much about things like fallen apples, and putting them to finish ripening in a warm conservatory, took Bill's advice and picked up some of the apples. During the day, the big windows of the conservatory, where Roderick wrote stories, made the place warm from the sun's rays even at this time of year. The apples would do well.

He made sure that the ones he picked up were not going bad, then he started off across the big lawn towards the house. A grey-white worm, having been disturbed from his afternoon sleep by Roderick picking up its particular apple, poked its head out of one of the apples – Roderick saw the worm and gasped then quickly placed the apple back on the ground and turned away. He did not like worms. The worm took a little bite of apple and went back to sleep.

Bill called after Roderick: "Be careful to put those apples up on the top of the cupboard. You don't want the mice to get at them before you do."

Roderick turned and, looking a little unsure of himself, remarked: "Mice? Mice, Bill? What are you talking about? There are no mice living in the house!"

Bill, who knew about this sort of thing, still muttering away to nobody in particular, went back to mowing the grass. "That's what you think, there's mice aplenty in yon house – always have been, always will be."

Roderick made his way across the big lawn and went up the steps of the conservatory as the old cathedral clock began to "donk" the hour.

Under the steps that led up and into the conservatory of the old house something stirred...

Hamish McMoosie was still in his bed when he heard the cathedral clock chime the hour. He started to count the donging. It was more of a "donk" than a "dong" because the great bell that tolled the hours had been cracked for over fifty years. He started to count but he felt just a little too sleepy to be really bothered. He decided to pull his tartan duvet back over his head and snuggle back down to sleep again.

The McMoosie home, snuggled under the conservatory of the old house, was considered by most mice folk in the Old City to be one of the most tranquil places to live. That was until Hamish started to practise on his pipes, and then tranquillity joined the swifts and went to Spain. Hamish's practices even made the bees stop work and put on bee earmufflers, which was a very unusual thing for bees to do. Nevertheless, Hamish McMoosie was recognised by all mice folk as being the county's best piper.

Hamish had had a very busy time the night before, playing his bagpipes with the Keltic Moosie Pipe and Fiddle Band over in the cathedral crypt. The occasion had been the wedding supper of his niece Flora McMoosie and her new husband Willie MacBridie, from the next town, south on the main road to Edinburgh. It was traditional for all the McMoosies to wed in the cathedral and to hold the supper and ceilidh in the crypt. The Minister Genesis MacBrimstone, held a wonderful service. All in all it was a very grand affair.

The McMoosie clan had gathered from far and wide. Even old Aunt Maude McMoosie, who rarely left her home in Edzell Castle, had travelled by bus the whole six miles to the old city to be at Flora's wedding. Of course being Aunt Maude McMoosie, she came with her umbrella!

Hamish and his wife Dorma, living as they did right next to the cathedral, invited Aunt Maude to stay the night with them, as the last bus for Edzell left far too early for any self respecting McMoosie to leave a ceilidh.

Hamish snuggled in his bed and thought about the ceilidh …

When all the dancing and partying had finished – just as the cathedral clock had donked twelve donks at midnight – Aunt Maude, Hamish and Dorma had walked home across the moonlit kirkyard. The pale yellow moon, shining in the cloudless night sky had cast long shadows of the yew bushes across the path in the cathedral grounds. An owl had hooted somewhere in the nearby woods and the eerie sound had echoed from the cold stone walls of the old cathedral.

Aunt Maude had led the way along the path from the great door of the cathedral, grasping her long, rolled up black umbrella with the carved head of a goose on the handle. She never went anywhere without her umbrella.

Aunt Maude had an unfortunate habit of poking people with the sharp end of the umbrella to get their attention if she thought that they were not listening to her. Hamish, who had been wobbling, just a little bit, had followed along behind Dorma and Aunt Maude. He had been ever so slightly staggering from perhaps a little too much damson wine, and he had made sure he kept out of range of Aunt Maude's long, black umbrella with the goose-head handle. He rubbed his bottom with one hand remembering the pain of many encounters with the sharp end.

Unfortunately, Hamish had been thinking too much about avoiding the sharp end of Aunt Maude's umbrella when he had tripped over a shadow and accidentally buried his head in a moonlit flower border.

"Hamish, stop falling over things, get up out of those flowers and come along at once!" Aunt Maude called out over her shoulder.

Hamish picked himself up from the flower border, and blew away a rose petal, that had somehow attached itself to his whiskers – he ambled along behind Dorma and Aunt Maude towards the house. He was in a very happy Hamish state of mind.

When they had reached their little home hidden under the steps of the conservatory of the old house, Dorma, Hamish's wife, bustled around the kitchen and soon had three steaming mugs of hot chocolate ready for them to sip in their beds. Hamish meanwhile, still being ever so slightly tipsy from perhaps just a little too much damson wine, had dropped his bagpipes down by the comfortable red leather sofa in the sitting room. He had been much too tired to put them away in their box.

Hamish was intending to put them away in the morning but he was even too tired to finish the mug of chocolate and Abernethy biscuit that Dorma put on the bedside table. All he wanted to do was sleep. The last thing he had heard was Aunt Maude's voice calling out from her bedroom, "Hamish! I want to be up at six o'clock sharp in the morning – six mind you. Tea would be nice, and a biscuit. And, Hamish, try not to snore!"

Somewhere far, far away and among the echoing "donks" from the cathedral clock Hamish heard the voice of Dorma calling to him. "Surely, it was not morning already?" he asked himself? Hamish thought to himself: "Was that ten "donks" I counted or was it six?" Suddenly, now slightly more awake Hamish realised the truth, and sadly remarked to the pillow, "Oh bother!" It was ten! Aunt Maude had wanted to be called at six! Before he had time to reply, Dorma's voice called again: "Hamish! Hamish, get out of that bed this minute. It's after ten o'clock and Aunt Maude has to catch the eleven o'clock bus to Edzell. If she misses the bus it will mean you taking her home in the car. Hamish!"

"Bother Aunt Maude," Hamish murmured to himself while still in the wonderful state of being half asleep now and knowing full well what time of day it was – having just heard the clock "donk" ten. He did not want to face the day, not just yet. Another five minutes perhaps even ten in bed would do no harm.

"Bother, Aunt Maude. In fact double bother," murmured Hamish, sleepily trying to ease himself lower and lower under the warm duvet. However, he thought better of it and called out in answer to the voice of Dorma: "I'm up my dear, I'm up. Tell Auntie that I will take her to Edzell, she will not have to catch the eleven o'clock bus."

Hamish hoped that his offer would delay his getting up by at least another five minutes. He snuggled down again and sighed: "Double bother Aunt Maude."

Hamish nearly jumped out of his skin when Dorma, who had silently glided into the bedroom without her husband knowing, whipped the duvet from over his half-asleep form.

"Hamish. Get up!"

Knowing when he was beaten, Hamish was out of the bed like a cork popping from a bottle. He ran into the bathroom, unscrewed the top from a tube of MacTrossach's special cheese-flavoured toothpaste for mice and spread his electric toothbrush with a thick blob of it. He then buzzed the toothbrush over his teeth; pulled off his tartan night-shirt; jumped under the shower, quickly scrubbing himself under the hot jet of water with his favourite apricot-and-haggis perfumed soap; slipped into a clean yellow roll-neck jumper and buckled on his kilt in less time than it takes to say: "Double bother Aunt Maude."

Hamish looked in the mirror and was pleased with the reflection he saw looking back at him. He gave his whiskers a tweak and smiled a little Hamish smile. He ran down the stairs full of Hamish glee and giggly Hamish thoughts.

Aunt Maude was waiting in the sitting room, tapping her right foot on the carpet, with, I might add, an air of some impatience, when the clean and bright Hamish popped his head round the door.

"Ready, Aunt ..."

Something he saw made his blood run cold! Hamish's voice died in his throat, his chest heaved, his heart started to beat at double its normal rate, his ears grew paler and paler until they were a chalky white. Hamish's mouth dropped open as he stared at the terrible sight that met his eyes.

Aunt Maude was standing by the very comfortable red leather sofa, her long black umbrella held aloft with the sharp pointed end uppermost. Hamish's eyes followed along Aunt Maude's raised arm, along the length of the long, black umbrella with the goose head handle, right to the tip of the pointed end which protruded through and out the other side of . . . the bag of his bagpipes! Aunt Maude had skewered his pipes! They were ruined. They would never, wail again. Never again would he be able to play the "Cheese Cutters' Jig".

A single tear drop formed at the corner of one of Hamish's big brown eyes and was soon joined by another and then another until a little river of tears ran down his face.

"Hamish!" Aunt Maude roared, looking at him over the tops of her glasses. "Hamish, these bagpipes have found themselves attached to my umbrella. Kindly remove them."

Hamish took his bagpipes from Aunt Maude and placed them, still attached to the umbrella, gently on the floor. With the care of a surgeon performing a delicate operation, Hamish, avoiding the goose-head handle, removed the bagpipes from the long, black umbrella. He thought he heard a soft plaintive sob from the pipes as he pulled the umbrella out of the bag, but he was not sure, perhaps it was just the wind sighing in the trees outside. Who can tell?

Hamish held the bagpipes with both hands and looked down at the limp fabric. He shook his head in sorrow, "My pipes, my pipes. What am I going to do?" He sobbed quietly to himself.

One of the teardrops ran along a drooping whisker and fell with a silent plop onto the carpet. "What am I going to do?" he asked himself. "What am I going to do?"

He was a piper without a set of pipes.

Aunt Maude, who was swiftly running out of patience, tapped her right foot – never a good sign as far as Hamish was concerned.

"Hamish, it's time we were off to Edzell. I have most certainly missed the bus. Stop standing there looking so miserable. Give me my umbrella."

Hamish did as he was told to do and handed over the umbrella. Aunt Maude peered through her glasses. "Let me see, I hope your bagpipes have not damaged my favourite umbrella. Why you are making such a face? They were only a set of old bagpipes, you'll just have to buy another set."

With that, Aunt Maude flounced from the sitting room, clutching the long, black umbrella with the goose-head handle. Hamish was not quite sure, but he thought that the umbrella sort of sneered at him as Aunt Maude went out of the room, but as he remarked to himself afterwards, it was most likely to be just a trick of the light or the result of the tears blurring his vision. But then, one could never tell with umbrellas.

Hamish sighed as he picked up his car keys … surely there were not any more umbrellas belonging to Aunt Maude he thought to himself – and then shuddered at the very idea – but she did say "favourite". Oh double bother, Aunt Maude.

From outside the sitting room and far down the long hall towards the front door he heard Aunt Maude's raised voice.

"Dorma, you will just have to take Hamish in hand! I do not know what he is thinking about at times. I just do not. Why, even now he is still in the sitting room, knowing I have to get home to Edzell Castle to feed the goldfish (who did not care very much for bagpipes, as they thought that bagpipes were so noisy and made the water in their bowl ripple). I really do despair." She turned her attention to poor Hamish: "Hamish! I am waiting to go home."

Aunt Maude got in the back seat of the car with her carpetbag and put her long, black umbrella with the goose-head handle on the front passenger seat next to Hamish. The journey home to Edzell Castle was completed in silence apart from Aunt Maude telling Hamish not to drive too fast, when to overtake tractors and to watch out for bicycles and straying Highland cows. For someone who had never had a driving lesson in her life, Aunt Maude knew a lot about driving.

Sometimes, out of the corner of his eye, Hamish thought he saw the umbrella sneering at him. How he hated that umbrella! Hamish was glad when they reached Edzell Castle. Aunt Maude and her long, black umbrella with the goose head handle removed themselves from the four by four.

Aunt Maude had snatched up her carpetbag, grasped her umbrella under her arm and, with a very brief goodbye to Hamish, marched up the castle drive and into her home. The big oak door to the castle slammed behind Aunt Maude as she entered carrying carpetbag and umbrella.

It seemed a long, lonely drive home for Hamish but when he got back Dorma was waiting for him with a kind smile. She had taken his bagpipes through to the kitchen and put them on the big table. Dorma was very good with a needle and thread and she had been trying to repair the tear in the bagpipes. However, even with all her skills, she found the damage to the bagpipes could not be repaired. Hamish looked at the pipes and gave Dorma a big hug as a thank you for trying to mend his bagpipes.

Dorma made them both a cup of tea and put out a plate of Hamish's favourite Abernethy biscuits. Now and again, Hamish could sometimes find an answer to a problem when he had eaten an Abernethy. (At least that is what he told everybody). They sat quietly in the warm, cosy kitchen.

There was a sudden excited squeak from Hamish's side of the table and Dorma did not say a thing when Hamish dunked his Abernethy in his tea before saying: "I know what to do! I will go and see what Alistair MacBrymer, the Bagpipe maker, has to say about my pipes – he is sure to come up with something".

There was a splittery, splattery, splashing plop as the soggy part of the dunked Abernethy, which Hamish had been lifting to his mouth, took a dive into Hamish's mug of tea and disappeared under the surface.

"Double bother," said Hamish – but with a happy smile he reached out for another biscuit.

Even Dorma could not be cross with him for dunking today.

"Double bother, indeed Hamish," said Dorma smiling.

Glossary

Abernethy	A traditional and popular Scottish biscuit first made to a Recipe of Dr Abernethy. Hamish's favourite served with a cup of tea and "dunked".
Brechin	An old cathedral city in the county of Angus, Scotland.
Brechin cathedral	A cathedral dating back almost 1000 years. Noted for its fine Pictish tower.
ceilidh	A Gaelic word (pronounced "kay-lee") for a Scottish party with traditional singing, dancing, folk music, storytelling and fun.
Edzell Castle	An ancient castle six miles from Brechin. Home of Aunt Maude
yon	A Scots word meaning 'that'.
kirk	A Scots word meaning 'church'.
kirkyard	A Scots word meaning 'churchyard'.

Dorma's Abernethy Biscuits

This recipe has an especially buttery taste which Hamish loves

5 ounces of plain flour
4 ounces of best Scottish butter
3 tablespoons of sugar
1 teaspoon of cream of tartar
Half a teaspoon of bicarbonate of soda
1 tablespoon of milk
1 pinch of salt

Sift the flour, salt, bicarbonate of soda and cream of tartar together. Rub in the butter to the flour mixture until the mixture looks like bread crumbs. Stir the sugar into the milk until it dissolves and then add it to the flour and butter mixture. Form the mixture into a stiff dough. Roll out the biscuit dough on a lightly floured board to a thickness of about half a centimetre and cut out 10 round shapes with a plain cutter. Prick each biscuit all over with a fork. Place the biscuits on a greased baking tray. Bake in a pre-heated oven at 350°F or 180°C for 15 minutes.

Enjoy!

Note: In Dr Abernethy's original 19th century recipe he added caraway seeds to the Abernethies which were said to help digestion. If you want to do this add about half a level teaspoon of caraway seeds to the flour mix.